For Lois Melman, Linda Jo Platt, and
Judith Michael . . . and for our bears!
—A. S. C.

For Andy, Joe, Matti, and Abi,
with my love always
—L. H.

Henry Holt and Company, LLC
Publishers since 1866
175 Fifth Avenue, New York, New York 10010
mackids.com

Library of Congress Cataloging-in-Publication Data
Capucilli, Alyssa Satin.
Not this bear / Alyssa Satin Capucilli ; illustrated by Lorna Hussey. — First edition.
pages   cm
Summary: "It's Bear's first day of school, and he's a bit reluctant to go. Mama says all bears love school;
Bear isn't so sure. But school turns out to be full of fun—painting pictures, listening to stories, and making
new friends. Maybe this bear will like school after all."—Provided by publisher
ISBN 978-0-8050-9896-9 (hardcover)
[1. First day of school—Fiction. 2. Schools—Fiction. 3. Bears—Fiction.]
I. Hussey, Lorna, illustrator. II. Title.
PZ7.C179No 2015   [E]—dc23   2014028525

Henry Holt books may be purchased for business or promotional use. For information on bulk purchases,
please contact the Macmillan Corporate and Premium Sales Department at
(800) 221-7945 x5442 or by e-mail at specialmarkets@macmillan.com.

First Edition—2015 / Designed by Ashley Halsey
The artist used watercolor, watercolor inks, and graphite on watercolor paper
to create the illustrations for this book.
Printed in China by Toppan Leefung Printing Ltd., Dongguan City, Guangdong Province

1 3 5 7 9 10 8 6 4 2

NOT THIS BEAR

Alyssa Satin Capucilli
Illustrated by Lorna Hussey

Henry Holt and Company
New York

It was Bear's first day of school. Mama gave Bear an extra big hug and an extra big kiss. Bear held on to Mama tightly.

"I will be waiting right by this tree for you," said Mama. "Have fun, Bear. All the bears love school."

"Not this bear," said Bear. He loved days at home with Mama.

Bear looked around the classroom.
He saw an easel filled with colorful paints.

"Would you like to paint, Bear?" asked Mr. Brown.

Bear nodded.

"You can hang your jacket in the cubby and put on a smock, just like the other bears," said Mr. Brown.

"Not this bear," said Bear. He wanted to hold on to his jacket just a bit longer.

So Mr. Brown helped
Bear with a smock.
And Bear held his
jacket under his arm
while he painted.

He painted a sun,

he painted a picture of Mama,

and he painted himself, too.

Soon it was time for a story.

"You may choose a mat, Bear.

All the bears like to sit on a mat and

listen to a story," said Mr. Brown.

"Not this bear," said Bear. He liked to sit on a comfy lap to hear a story. But he chose a mat, and then he found a small bunny to sit on his lap. It was a very good story.

Snack time was next.

"Every bear likes a snack at school," said Mr. Brown.

"Not this bear," said Bear. Mama always made the best snacks of all. Still, it was fun to help pour the juice and to pass out the napkins.

And when Mr. Brown cut an apple in half, there
was a beautiful star! Bear had never seen that before.

Bear built a tall tower of blocks.

He dressed up like a pirate.

He stirred and mixed in the kitchen.

He even gave the
baby doll a bath.

"You are being very careful not to get soap in
the doll's eyes, Bear," said Mr. Brown. "Good job!"
Bear smiled. Mama was always careful not
to get soap in his eyes.

Before long, it was time to go to the playground.

"This way, Bear," said Mr. Brown. "All the bears love to run and swing and slide!"

"Not this bear," said Bear.
"Not this bear, either,"
said another bear.

So they made rainbows with chalk,

and they blew bubbles that
popped on their noses,

and they rode shiny tricycles around
and around and around,

until Mr. Brown said, "Are you ready to go home, Bear?"

"Not this bear!" said Bear. "School is fun!"

"I'm so glad you feel that way," said Mr. Brown. "I will see you tomorrow."

Mama was waiting by the tree,
just like she said she would.
"I can't wait to hear about your
day at school, Bear," said
Mama. "This bear really
missed you."

Bear gave Mama an extra big hug and an extra big kiss. He showed Mama his painting.

"This bear missed you, too," said Bear.

31192020794267